Quantum Squeak

Quantum Squeak

Mary Hoffman

Illustrated by Anthony Lewis

ORCHARD BOOKS

For Sarah Debenham,
reader and friend

ORCHARD BOOKS
96 Leonard Street, London EC2A 4RH
Orchard Books Australia
14 Mars Road, Lane Cove, NSW 2066
ISBN 1 86039 479 5
First published in Great Britain 1996
First paperback publication 1997
Text © Mary Hoffman 1996
Illustrations © Anthony Lewis 1996
The right of Mary Hoffman to be identified as the author and
Anthony Lewis as the illustrator of this
work has been asserted by them in accordance with the Copyright,
Designs and Patents Act, 1988.
A CIP catalogue record for this book is available from the British
Library.
Printed in Great Britain

Contents

1

Jurassic Lark

Cedric was doing his exercises. These were not of the ordinary keep-fit sort because, firstly, Cedric was a mouse and, secondly, it was his magical powers he was flexing rather than his muscles. Cedric was no ordinary pet mouse, though he did belong to a master – two in fact. He was the seventeenth son of a seventeenth son and a magician's familiar. A familiar is an animal that helps its master with spells, but Cedric preferred to think of himself as a sort of apprentice, or magician with L-plates. The white mouse also belonged to a boy called Alex, who lived in the same house as the magician. Or, to be more accurate, the magician lived in Alex's house; he was a lodger in the Brodies' attic.

Cedric flexed his front paws and woffled his
whiskers. Slowly his little body rose several inches
into the air. At that moment the door crashed open
and Alex burst in. Cedric fell quickly back on to the
floor of his cage.

"Do you mind?" said the mouse crossly. "I was
just getting the hang of levitation."

"Sorry, Cedric," said Alex. "Why were you
doing that?"

"A magician must practise his basic spells regu-
larly," said Cedric, "or he doesn't have the power

at his disposal when it comes to doing really serious magic."

"And how are you getting on with the serious magic?" asked Alex. He and Cedric were plotting something which required some very serious magic indeed. Alex's younger sister Carrie was coming up to her birthday, which always made her sad. The only present she wanted was the one she couldn't have – a cat of her own. The only one she had ever had that she could stroke and cuddle was Beauty the tortoiseshell, and that cat had been a ghost. Carrie's asthma meant that a real living furry cat was something she couldn't have for many years – if ever.

It was Cedric who had solved the problem, temporarily, by bringing Carrie a ghost cat, among a lot of other animals from the past. Alex, who loved animals just as much as Carrie did, still had fond memories of his own pair of ghostly wolfhounds. But Cedric's magician, Mungo, had forbidden him to try the ghost spell again. The mouse had had quite a success with an invisibility spell that summer, but although it had given the children some good adventures, including catching a gang of burglars, it hadn't helped Carrie with cats. She was still affected by their fur, even when she was invisible.

Now Cedric, with Alex's encouragement, was working on a new spell. It was to be Alex's birthday present to Carrie. "If the mountain won't come to Mahomet, Mahomet must go to the mountain," he had said when Alex asked if there was any way to get Carrie and Beauty back together again.

"What does that mean?" asked Alex.

"Time travel," said Cedric.

That had been three days ago and ever since then Cedric had been scuttling his way through Mungo's library of spell books and doing his magical gymnastics in preparation for taking the children back in time. It was a lot harder than the other two spells had been and he wasn't at all sure he could manage it. Cedric's magic was a bit hit and miss at the best of times and there was just so *much* of the past. He was pretty confident that he could take the children back, but whether he could aim them properly to arrive at the ten or so years of Beauty's life, during the second world war, was another matter.

But Cedric was a proud and boastful mouse who never liked to admit what he didn't know about magic and spells. It was only two days until Carrie's birthday and he was determined not to let Alex down.

Carrie's present from Alex looked ordinary enough. It was a paperback book in a series about horses she was collecting and she would have been pleased if that had been all it was. But Alex had written on his gift-tag "see page 20, don't tell parents" and, when Carrie turned to that page, she found a mysterious note. "I.O.U. one spell," it said. "Collect at midnight, my room." Carrie was very puzzled but she tried not to show it. After all, although their parents did not know that their lodger was a magician or that Alex's mouse was a familiar, they did get sort of nervous whenever magic was going on in the house.

By midnight, Carrie was quite sleepy, after her party and going to see a film with friends, but she wasn't going to miss out on her last present, particularly when it was a spell. She crept quietly along to Alex's room and knocked softly on the door.

"Oh, you're in your pyjamas," said Alex, when he let her in.

"Yes, I was getting ready for bed," said Carrie. "It doesn't matter, does it? I mean will the spell take long?"

"No-o-oh," said Alex, looking at Cedric who was nervously fussing up and down the bed rail. "Only we might have to go out of doors."

"That's all right," said Carrie. "I'm wearing my dressing gown and slippers."

"Well, there's no time to change, anyway," said Alex, who was still fully dressed in jeans and a sweatshirt with his jacket on top. "Cedric's ready. Aren't you?"

"Of course," snapped Cedric. "Now come and stand here, you two. And you'd better hold hands."

"Aren't you going with us?" said Alex, suddenly a bit alarmed about how they were going to get back to the present from the 1940s.

"Yes, yes, I'll come," said Cedric. "But you and Carrie mustn't get separated."

"Where are we going?" asked Carrie, round-eyed. "Is it going to be like when we were invisible?"

"Wait and see," grinned Alex. "OK, Cedric. Ready for blast-off!"

The two children held hands and Cedric climbed into Alex's top jacket pocket, his favourite place. The mouse peered out from under the flap, waved his front paws and made a series of unintelligible squeaks. All around them, the familiar objects of Alex's bedroom began to fade. His bed and chest of drawers became see-through, just as Alex himself had once been when the invisibility spell misbehaved. His football and music posters disappeared from the walls, then the walls themselves were no longer there. Finally the floor went and the two children stood on nothing. All around them was a rushing sound and streaks of black, green and white. Although they were standing quite still, they had the impression of travelling at a terrifyingly fast rate. Instinctively, they closed their eyes to stop themselves feeling dizzy.

When they opened them again they were indeed outside, but it was daylight and so warm that it didn't matter that Carrie was in her night things. Everything around them was lush and green in the bright sunlight. It was a marshy area with huge brightly coloured dragonflies darting about.

"Cedric," hissed Alex. "We're not going to find Beauty here. It's somewhere in the country."

"It's beautiful, Alex," said Carrie, before the mouse could answer. "And it's so clever of Cedric. A lovely outing to the country in the summer, when it's cold and dark autumn at home. I've never had my birthday on a really sunny day before. Thank you."

She had let go of Alex's hand and wandered down to a river bank. There were frogs in the water and lizards on the bank. Alex began to feel nervous. This wasn't right for London in the second world war. He was sure they didn't have lizards even then.

"Oh look, Alex!" cried Carrie. "There's a turtle!"

And there was, a huge dark green one sculling lazily through the water. Alex went to join Carrie on the bank.

"And there's something else," said Carrie, peering at the water. Suddenly she went very white and clutched Alex's arm. "It's a crocodile!" she said.

15

The ancient scaly creature raised its head a fraction out of the water and looked at the children with unblinking yellow eyes. It started to swim towards the bank.

"Quickly, run," said Alex and as they ran, crashing their way through rocks and ferns into a forest of trees they didn't recognise, he moaned, "Where on earth are we, Cedric? This wasn't what was supposed to happen at all!"

When they were far enough from the river to be sure the crocodile wasn't following them, they flung themselves on the forest floor, panting. The sun streamed in through the tops of trees. There were ones that looked a bit like monkey-puzzles, others like tall pineapples and some that looked like ferns stuck on top of tall stalks.

"There's something funny about this wood," said Carrie, sitting up. "You can't hear any birds."

It was indeed eerily silent. Then Alex noticed something at the top of one of the tall fern trees.

"Look," he said, "there's some kind of parrot up there. Cedric's brought us to a jungle I think."

The parrot suddenly flipped down from the tree.

It didn't exactly fly, more glided like a squirrel. As it landed on a lower branch nearer the children it opened its beak and gave a raucous squawk. Alex gulped. It had teeth. He looked more closely. There were three large claws on each of its wings. It wasn't a big bird, it was no bigger than a magpie, but seeing it there and suddenly knowing what it was made Alex freeze with fear. He got up slowly and moved as casually as he could out of Carrie's earshot.

"Cedric!" he said. "What have you done?"

"I seem to have overshot the second world war and gone back a bit too far," said the mouse guiltily.

"Overshot?" said Alex. "I'd say that was the understatement of the year! That creature over there, which Carrie thinks is a nice parrot, is an archaeopteryx! You've gone back at least a hundred and fifty million years. You've taken us back to the time of the dinosaurs, you idiot!"

"That's not very grateful, is it?" said the mouse indignantly.

"All I asked for was a short stroll down memory lane, so Carrie would see her cat again, not a trip back to prehistory. Now, just get us back home as fast as you can, before Carrie guesses. We might come face to face with a meat-eating dinosaur the size of a double-decker bus!"

Cedric coughed. "Er, I'm not entirely sure that I can."

At that moment the ground began to shake and the forest filled with the sound of enormous foot-steps.

2

The Sands of Time

Alex tried desperately to remember all he knew about dinosaurs. His dinosaur phase, when he knew all the names and even how to spell them, had been over some years ago. His 'swamp' full of stones and plastic models of dinosaurs had been thrown out of the loft when it was converted for Mungo the magician. But although it contained stegosaurs and triceratops, diplodocus and Tyrannosaurus rex, Alex really knew that these monster lizards come from times millions of years apart.

"Think, think!" Alex told himself. "That's definitely Archaeopteryx in the tree, so this must be some Jurassic forest. If there's a big dinosaur coming, it can't be Tyrannosaurus."

"What is it, Alex?" cried Carrie, still unaware of the danger.

"I think Cedric's taken us a bit too far back, Carrie," said Alex much more casually than he felt. "It's probably some kind of dinosaur. But don't worry. Cedric's doing a spell to get us back home."

At that moment a group of about half a dozen dinosaurs broke through the trees, They were about four feet tall and they ran on their long back legs. They were obviously running away from something. The group parted round the tree where Alex and Carrie stood and kept running without taking any notice of them.

"Oh!" gasped Carrie. "They really are dinosaurs."

She seemed almost as pleased as if they had been cats. But Alex knew that though these might be some harmless plant-eaters – dryosaurs perhaps – what was chasing them must be both big and meat-eating. Its normal diet would never have contained humans but it wasn't likely to be picky about food.

"Cedric!" Alex whispered urgently. "The spell!"

"All right, all right," said the flustered mouse. "I think I've got it. I've had to make adjustments because we're a bit further back in time than I thought we would be."

Alex would have had something to say about that, but just then the trees parted and a lizard the size of a double-decker bus burst into the clearing.

"It's a T rex!" whispered Carrie.

"No, it's not," said Alex in what he hoped was a calm voice. "It's an Allosaurus. T Rex was much later."

"That's all right then," said Carrie and gulped.

Alex grasped her hand firmly and scuttled behind the tree. The footsteps were coming nearer. It was the only sound. The giant lizard did not roar like a dinosaur in a special effects film. It just moved steadily closer to the tree behind which the children were hiding.

"Cedric!" pleaded Alex.

The tree began to tremble, as if the dinosaur had taken hold of it and was shaking it to see if it contained food. Alex and Carrie closed their eyes and tried to believe this was a nightmare they were going to wake up from very soon.

When they opened them again, it seemed as if the pretence had worked. They weren't in a forest with a hungry carnivorous dinosaur any more. But on the other hand, they clearly weren't in Alex's bedroom in Ferry Road either. They were standing on warm sand beside a very wide river. The sun wasn't high in the sky yet but it was obvious that it would be a very hot day indeed when it got there.

"Thanks, Cedric," said Alex, breathing out a bit. "That was a nasty moment."

"Where are we?" said Carrie, who was beginning to find her fluffy dressing gown a bit warm. "It doesn't look like Edinburgh."

"A-hum," said the mouse.

"You don't know, do you?" said Alex wearily.

Then Carrie gave a small scream and pointed at the water.

"There's crocodiles here too! I don't believe he's taken us away from the dinosaurs at all. We're just in a different part!"

Alex was just trying to remember what kind of dinosaurs lived in deserts when he saw something on the horizon that definitely wasn't a reptile of any kind. A string of camels was coming their way.

"Phew!" breathed Alex in relief. He didn't know

23

how long camels had been on the earth but he did know they hadn't been about in Jurassic times. "It's all right, Carrie," he said. "We're nowhere prehistoric. We might even be in the right time."

"But we're not in the right place," objected Carrie. "Didn't you say Cedric was taking us home?"

Since they didn't seem to have any choice, the children waited for the camel train to arrive. Carrie took off her dressing gown and Alex his jacket and they spread them on the sand and sat on them. Cedric lay in Alex's hand, totally exhausted by their escape from prehistory.

As the camel riders came closer, it was clear they

were wearing white, but not the flowing robes of desert Arabs. They were all men and they seemed to be wearing short pleated skirts. They had brown skins and black hair and talked in a language the children couldn't understand. There were only about six men, leading two dozen camels. The men were very well organised, six of them taking two camels at a time down to the river where the ungainly animals splayed out their front legs and put their muzzles into the water for a long drink. The other three men stayed with the camels who hadn't yet had their turn, calming them down as they made excited bubbling noises in their throats. When nearly all the camels had drunk, two men took pottery jars down to the water up river from where the animals were drinking and started to fill them. No one noticed the children; it was a bit like when they had been invisible.

Cedric stirred in Alex's hand and opened his eyes. "Did I do it?" he asked. "Did I save you from the dinosaur?"

"Yes," said Alex, "but you didn't get us home."

Cedric sat up and looked round at the desert scene. "Oh dear," he said. "Nor I did. This seems to be Ancient Egypt."

"We can't understand what they're saying," said Carrie.

"I think I can do something to help with that," said Cedric. "I know a spell that acts like a translator. If I do it, you'll be able to understand them and they'll be able to understand you."

"I don't know that they can even *see* us," said Alex. "But do the spell anyway. Only I hope you really can do it and it won't turn us into camels or something."

Cedric looked pained and muttered something under his breath.

"Better be getting back," said the camel driver nearest to the children. "Old Nahkten knows to the minute how long it takes to water camels."

"Yeah," agreed the other man, "and if we're a minute longer, he'll knock it off our pay."

"Hang on!" exclaimed the first man, suddenly noticing the children. "What's this?"

All the camel drivers gathered round the children, scratching their heads and asking questions. Alex and Carrie couldn't easily answer any of them. They could give their names, although the Egyptians had trouble pronouncing them, but when they were asked where they had come from and how they had got there, Scotland conveyed nothing to the camel drivers. They didn't even attempt to explain that they had been brought back in time by a magic mouse, or rather forward from the time of the dinosaurs.

The chief camel driver quickly decided that the children should be taken to see Nahkten, who turned out to be his foreman, in order to explain the delay in their return. So Alex and Carrie were hoisted up, not unkindly, on to the hump of one of the quieter camels. There followed a very uncomfortable ride indeed.

The camel train went quite quickly, as the drivers tried to make up time. The pottery water jars tied to the camel saddle bumped heavily against the children's legs. The camel's movement was awkward and difficult to predict, so they were flung about a lot and were very glad that they had been tied to the saddle. In the circumstances, it was difficult to take much notice of their surroundings. At first it seemed as if there was nothing but sand and more sand in all directions. But after what seemed like ages of being bumped about, they could see in the distance some easily recognised shapes.

"Pyramids," gasped Alex.

"And that one's not finished," added Carrie.

The camel train came to a wheezing, moaning halt near what looked like a giant lumpy sand castle in front of a tall and most impressive pyramid.

Another man in a white pleated skirt, but with a wide blue collar round his neck, came forward to meet the chief camel driver. He looked annoyed, but when he saw Alex and Carrie his dark eyes widened in amazement.

"Found by the Nile?" he said. "Barbarian children?"

"We're not Barbarians," said Alex firmly, "we're Scottish."

But imagining how he and Carrie must look to the foreman, he had to admit privately they certainly looked different from all the people around them. His jeans and T-shirt printed with a 'Save the rainforest' logo, his navy trainers with white stars, his grey sweatshirt with Hearts of Midlothian emblazoned on it, were as alien to these white-skirted Egyptians as their garb would have been at a football match in Edinburgh. And as for Carrie, in her cat-patterned pyjamas and slippers with her fluffy blue dressing gown rolled in a bundle under her arm...

Nahkten leaned forward suddenly to peer at Carrie's clothes. Then he made a strange gesture and touched a tattoo on his bare chest which looked like an eye.

"My apologies," he said to Carrie. "I see, that though strangely garbed, you are a follower of the goddess Bastet. We do not wish to offend. Perhaps you are her priestess from a faraway land? But your slave cannot be allowed to walk around in those garments. Ani! See that the slave is given new clothes!"

Before Alex could protest, a boy about his own age, wearing a smaller blue collar like the foreman's, came forward and took him off to some workmen's huts. He turned round to see what was happening to Carrie, but everyone was treating her with great respect.

"Perhaps you would care to inspect the works?" said Nahkten, gesturing towards the great sand castle, which Carrie could now see was covered in long spindly ladders of different heights. Dozens of workmen, all dressed in pleated white skirts, were digging or brushing at the sand. It was as if they were trying to unearth something from under it. Now Carrie came to look at it, she could see that the shape was vaguely familiar – a long oblong in front of a tall oblong, with an even taller bit at the front of the second oblong, where the longest ladders were. A workman on the longest ladder suddenly gave a cry of surprise or triumph and pointed to something near the top of the highest lump on the sand castle. It was an eye.

"The sphinx," gasped Carrie. "It's the sphinx."

"Indeed you are a priestess of Bastet," said Nahkten, impressed. "It is the sphinx of the great Pharaoh Khafre, built over a thousand years ago."

"But why is it all covered with sand like that?" said Carrie, who had seen the sphinx and the great pyramids at Giza on any number of TV travel programmes and in travel agents' windows, and always clear of sand.

"My master, King Thutmose, may he ever prosper and reign in peace," said Nahkten, "had a dream, in which Harmachis, god of the rising sun, told him we must clear the sands of time from the old Pharaoh's sphinx. They have blown over the mighty statue from the desert for hundreds of years. King Thutmose says it is an omen. How can the Pharaoh rule strongly in Egypt while the lion – symbol of his power – lies buried in sand?"

Alex came out of the hut wearing a pleated skirt. He looked very sheepish. He was carrying his own clothes in a bundle.

"Ah, here is your slave!" said Nahkten. "Give him your extraordinary cloak to carry. One of my slaves will fan you as we walk along and others will bring refreshment. Ani! See to it."

Carrie looked anxiously for Cedric and saw him peeping out of Alex's clothes as she lay her blue fluffy 'cloak' on top of the pile.

Unfortunately, Nahkten saw him at the same time. The effect was sudden and electric."

"Ani! There's a grain-stealer in the slave's clothing! Quick, unleash the cats!"

Alex and Carrie exchanged horrified looks as the foreman's son ran to another sort of shed. Horrible yowling sounds followed as two beautiful sleek cats bolted out of the door and stopped to sniff the air. They were shaped a bit like Siameses and had very raucous voices. Their tails lashed from side to side and they looked lean and fit. At any other time Carrie would have been thrilled to see them. Even now she couldn't resist moving towards them. The cats stalked slowly to meet her.

"Cedric!" said Alex fiercely, "you are about to become a cat's dinner. If you don't get us back home right NOW, we soon won't be able to go anywhere."

Suddenly the sand of the desert began to fly blindingly around the two children like a stinging golden rain. It got into their eyes and nostrils and pricked their skin like a thousand tiny knives. The black hair of the Egyptians became dusted with gold as the children found themselves lifted into a whirlwind of sand. The pyramids dropped away below them till they looked like little molehills in the sand and then the world went black.

3

Mackindoe's Law

Alex tried to open his eyes but all he could see was millions of gold specks against blackness. He thought he'd try groaning for a bit, to see if that helped.

"They're coming round," said a familiar voice. He opened his eyes again and now saw red, the comforting well-known carroty-red of his best friend Ginger's fringe, which hung down over Ginger's worried eyes.

"Hi," said Alex weakly. "What are you doing in Ancient Egypt?"

"What are you doing in a pleated skirt?" said Ginger grinning. "And this isn't Ancient Egypt, even if you're dressed up like Cleopatra. It's your

room in Ferry Road."

"Where's Carrie?" asked Alex, struggling to sit up and finding his head still dizzy from his bird's eye view of the pyramids.

"She's here and quite safe," said another familiar voice. The sandy whiskers of Mungo the magician swam into view. Alex closed his eyes again; he didn't want to be reminded of sand. Then he opened them wide again. "What about Cedric?"

Mungo's large hand came up with a very weak-looking white mouse in it. Cedric opened one pink eye and gave a mouse-sized groan of his own.

"What happened?" asked Alex.

"What happened," said Ginger, "was your parents couldn't find either of you this morning so they rang me. I had to say I didn't know where you were, but I came round anyway. It was just like the summer, when you vanished."

"Where are they now?" asked Alex, anxiously.

"Searching the streets for you," said Mungo grimly. "But as soon as Ginger told me what was wrong, I suspected Cedric had something to do with it. I had to use some very strong magic indeed to bring you back from three and a half thousand years ago and thousands of miles away."

"Were you really in Ancient Egypt?" asked Ginger enviously. "I wish I'd been with you."

"We were back with the dinosaurs first," said Carrie, sounding a bit tired but otherwise normal.

"No kidding!" said Ginger. "You lucky devils."

"You wouldn't say that if you'd seen that big dinosaur that wanted to eat us," said Carrie. "It wasn't a special effect – it was real!"

"Do you know where we were then?" Alex asked Mungo.

"I had to trace the time and space pattern you'd travelled through, in order to find out where you had gone," said Mungo. "It would appear you were first somewhere in Utah about a hundred and fifty million years ago." He paused. "Would it be too much to ask you or Cedric where you were aiming for?"

Alex blushed. He always hated it when Cedric got the magic wrong and the children ended up having to be rescued. Mungo was the kindest man in the world as well as one of the best magicians ever, but Alex hated being made to look a fool in front of him.

"It was Carrie's birthday present," he said. "We were going to take her to see Beauty the cat, back in her own time."

"Oh, Alex," said Carrie. "That was a really sweet idea. I would've loved to see Beauty again." Suddenly she looked sad.

"Well, you still could," said Mungo.

All three children looked up at him expectantly.

Was time travel really going to be one of the spells that Mungo allowed?

"Oh no," groaned Cedric. "I don't want to go through anything like that again. Do you know those people actually *worshipped* cats? Because they were so good at catching mice! And there were two who were going to catch me!" He shuddered so dramatically that the children couldn't help laughing at him.

"I think what you all need is breakfast," said Mungo briskly, "including Cedric. And you, Alex, had better get out of your, er, interesting costume and back into your own clothes. Carrie, I think you had better get dressed too. It is always most unwise to travel time in one's night garments. And if your parents think you've been outdoors in your pyjamas, they're going to smell a rat."

"What *are* we going to tell Mum and Dad?" said Carrie.

"We can discuss that at breakfast," said Mungo. "And after that we can talk about the conventions of time travel."

*

"You see," said Mungo, up in his attic later that morning, "it can be very dangerous to tamper with the past. That's why I had to do an emergency spell to bring you back."

Alex and Carrie's parents had had to make do with the explanation that the children had gone out really early to the flower market to bring back a thank-you present for Carrie's birthday celebrations. Mungo had obligingly provided a huge bunch of flowers for Mrs Brodie and a handsome rhubarb plant for Mr Brodie's vegetable patch. Mrs Brodie couldn't help a tiny flicker of memory that the green jumper Carrie was now wearing had been on a chair in her room when she searched it earlier, but it guttered out under the golden gaze of Mungo Mackindoe.

"What sort of tampering?" asked Alex.

"Anything at all," said Mungo. "Suppose you had mentioned that the Sphinx had lost its nose. The workers might have been more careful in cleaning the sand off it and it would still be there today."

"Was that how it lost its nose?" asked Carrie.

"Why would it matter if it still had it?" said Ginger at the same time.

"It's just an example, Carrie," said Mungo. "I don't know how it happened. Why it would matter, Ginger, is that it would have dislodged a bit of history from its proper place. That way the whole of time since then would rearrange itself a tiny fraction to fit. It wouldn't be very noticeable for the first few hundred years, but by our time there might be a very big gap, waiting to be filled by a bit of alternative history."

"Like what?" said Alex.

"I don't know," said Mungo. "Maybe penicillin wouldn't have got invented."

"Would it have to be a bad thing?" said Carrie.

"No," said Mungo. "Maybe the atom bomb wouldn't have got invented. The point is, you don't *know* what the consequences would be. That's why it's so dangerous. We have to make the best of the history we've got, I'm afraid."

Alex thought for a bit. "Won't it have changed history a bit for two twentieth-century children to have visited the dinosaurs and ancient Egypt?"

Mungo laughed. "I don't think you made much impression on the dinosaurs. And as for the Egyptians, I expect there's a tablet somewhere full of hieroglyphs that puzzle scholars about a flying goddess associated with cats, and her slave who followed her up in the air. But you didn't do anything to alter what they were doing."

"Is it true about the Sphinx being covered with sand?" asked Ginger, who had heard the whole story while Mungo was creating fruit and flowers.

"Yes," said Mungo. "It was all dug off on the orders of Thutmose IV and it never came back."

"Can we really do time travel again?" asked Carrie. "If we don't do any tampering?"

Mungo looked at Cedric, who was fast asleep in the inkwell. "I don't want to stop all Cedric's attempts at magic," he said softly.

"He really is quite good, for a familiar. But time and space are vast and he's only a small mouse. He's certain to get things a bit wrong, I suspect. So I'm going to give you an insurance policy."

The children looked at one another. That didn't sound at all exciting. Mungo smiled.

"A word of power," he said. "Something to ensure that you can get back to your own time and space if things get difficult. But don't use it unless Cedric's in a real fix he can't get out of." Mungo leaned over to Alex and whispered a word in his ear. The syllables burned into Alex's brain. He would never forget a word like that, all made of fire and trumpets, and it stopped him from believing that Mungo thought he was a fool.

"Right," he said. Ginger looked a bit forlorn.

"Can Ginger come too?" asked Alex.

Mungo nodded.

"When can we go?" said Carrie. She couldn't wait to see Beauty again. But, as it happened, she was going to have a very long wait indeed.

To begin with, Cedric wasn't at all keen on trying time travel again and they weren't allowed to tell him about the insurance policy. It wasn't till the following weekend that he felt strong enough to attempt it again. The three children assembled in the Brodies' back garden, dressed for all eventualities. Each was wearing a T-shirt and cut-offs under a sweater and jeans, since they didn't know whether it would be hot or cold even if Cedric did take them where he was aiming. Alex carried his jacket with Cedric in the top pocket. Everyone had secretly pocketed various items useful to explorers which they hoped to produce triumphantly if there was a crisis. But this too they kept secret from Cedric. As far as he was concerned, they expected to be taken straight to Beauty and then home. He was not revealing any doubts to them either.

"All ready, then?" said the mouse brightly, and when they nodded began his incantation.

They held hands. Alex and Carrie had warned Ginger about the whirling sensation but when it came he was very glad he was holding on to them or he would have fallen. The Ferry Road garden disappeared in a blurring of white light.

When the whirling stopped, the first thing that

struck them was the freezing cold. The second thing was that the bright white light was still there. It was reflecting off the snow, which stretched all around them as far as the eye could see. They gasped with the cold and shivered in their thick fleecy-lined sweatshirts which had seemed too stuffy back in Edinburgh.

"Is this the North Pole?" asked Ginger, his teeth chattering. "I'm sure they didn't have the second world war up there."

"No," said Alex, "there's the sea."

What had seemed like continuous snow at first was countryside around a sea filled with ice-floes. As they trudged towards the coastline, their trainers soon soaking wet, they could see patches of blue water. At last they came to the top of a hill and looked down over a calm bay, a mixture of white and blue like the sky in the brilliant cold sunshine. But it wasn't the cold that took their breath away as they looked down. There, beached on the shore beneath them, lay a Viking longship.

4

A Northern Saga

"Uh-oh," said Ginger. "Vikings. That means raiders with ginger beards wearing helmets with horns."

"Ginger beard yourself," said Carrie tartly. "It's a myth about the horned helmets and they weren't all raiders."

Carrie considered herself something of an expert on Vikings. The year before she had constructed an elaborate Viking village out of a paper kit. It had occupied a huge tray in the dining-room for ages until it got dusty and Mrs Brodie had thrown it out.

"Look," said Alex, pointing. "There's your village, Carrie."

It was true. To the right of the ship, which dominated the view, were the turf roofs and log cabins of a Viking settlement. From where they were, the children could see tiny people streaming out of the wooden houses and running down to the shoreline to meet men climbing off the ship. It was just like seeing the paper village come alive. They could even see small sheep and cows.

Alex held Cedric up so he could view the scene beneath them. "What do you think?" he asked the mouse.

"Oh dear," said Cedric. "Still too far back. Though it's at least two and a half thousand years since the Egyptians. I didn't want to adjust the spell too much, in case we ended up in the future."

"But what do we do?" asked Alex. "Go back home or just try to go – let me see – about another nine hundred and forty years forward?" He was beginning to see how tricky it was to master time travel.

"No fear!" said Ginger, setting off down the hill. "We can't miss an adventure like this! We'll be the

47

only modern kids ever to see a real Viking warship. We've got to take a close look."

He was already out of earshot, slipping and sliding down the snowy hillside, when there came a shout from behind the children. A boy and girl about Alex's and Carrie's age were standing behind them and they held by a rope what was unmistakably a wooden sledge.

"Hullo," said the boy. "We'll get down quicker with this."

"Cedric must still have the translator spell switched on," whispered Carrie.

The children were wearing rough woollen clothes, with what looked like leather galoshes on their feet. Their cheeks glowed with the cold and the effort of having hauled their sledge up a different part of the hill. They wasted no time on introductions and didn't seem surprised at Alex and Carrie's appearance, but motioned them to get on the sledge, which was very big and sturdy. It was like a meeting in a dream. The four children hurtled down the air almost as dizzyingly as in a time leap. They overtook Ginger halfway down, who

threw them a startled look as the sledge went careening past. They landed in a heap on the snowy shore, panting and giggling. It was just like sledging at home and the Viking children might have been their own friends in the park near Ferry Road. Ginger joined them a few seconds later, having skidded most of the way down on his bottom.

"I am Magnus," said the Viking boy, "and this is my sister Ingvar."

"I am Alex, Alexander, really," said Alex, "and this is my sister, Carrie or Caroline, and this," as Ginger fell on top of him, "is my friend Ginger, though his real name's Gordon."

"You must come from a strange land indeed if everyone has two names," said Magnus. "We have other names too, but of our parents. Mine is Leifsson and Ingvar's is Gudrunsdottir."

Carrie giggled. "Then ours are Shirleysdaughter and Deriksson."

Magnus looked at Ginger. There was an awkward silence because Ginger did not know his father. Then a small voice squeaked: "He is known as Gordon the Red. That is what "Ginger" means where we come from."

Magnus and Ingvar looked as if their eyes would fall out as they stared at Cedric struggling out of Alex's pocket, where he had stuffed him for the mad tobogganing down the hill.

"Can all the animals talk where you come from?" asked Ingvar.

"No," said Carrie. "Only this one." She thought. "Allow us to introduce Cedric Cedricsson, otherwise known as Cedric the White. He knows how to do magic."

The two Viking children stood up and bowed.

Then they started brushing sand and snow off their clothes.

"Come, Alex Deriksson, Carrie Shirleysdottir and Gordon the Red, we must go to greet the seafarers. Our father, Leif Magnusson, was on that ship."

The children needed no second invitation. All fear of horned raiders gone, they ran towards the mighty wooden ship beached on the shore, which was now surrounded by excited villagers. Many men from the ship were clasping women and children in big bearhugs. They all seemed to be very big and burly. Some indeed had ginger beards, but the one that Magnus and Ingvar ran to greet was a black-haired giant, his beard just touched with silver, like icing sugar sprinkled on a chocolate cake. He had one broad arm round a tall dark-haired woman but easily scooped the two children up in his other one.

"Welcome home, Father," said Magnus in a muffled voice. "Did you find land?"

"We did indeed," said Leif, setting his children down. "A fine land full of fruit and corn. I'll tell you all about it as soon as we've unloaded and got back to the village. We are longing for fresh meat and bread without weevils that doesn't break our teeth!" He laughed, showing his fine white teeth, which looked quite unscathed by sailors' rations.

"These are our new friends," said Ingvar, pointing to the time travellers. "They come from the land of Two Names and they have a magic animal."

Ingvar's mother, Gudrun, looked a bit suspicious of these new 'friends' she had never seen before, but Leif just laughed all the harder.

"The imagination of our daughter, Gudrun! I think she will be a skald when she grows up and write sagas to keep us entertained on the long winter nights."

There was a great bustle then to unload the ship and reunite families. The sailors had obviously been away for a long time and seemed more like explorers than warriors. They had swords in their belts, but they didn't wear armour. There was much talk of the new land they had discovered, as the children mingled among the villagers.

"They say that the Chief has stayed behind to start a settlement there," said one woman to her friend.

"Yes, and that he calls it Vineland, because of all the fruit that grows there," said the other.

Alex had an idea. "What do you call this country you live in?" he asked Magnus.

The boy looked at him curiously.

"It is a strange traveller who doesn't know the country he's visiting," he said. "We are not like those wild places my father has just come from. This is the Green Land, called that throughout the Countries of the North."

"It doesn't *look* very green," objected Ginger, looking at all the snow.

"Wait till the summer and you will see," said Magnus stiffly and went off to help his father.

"Greenland *is* all ice and snow, silly," said Carrie. "Didn't they call it that to make it seem nicer, so more people would go and live there?"

"I think I know what Vineland may be too," said Alex, "though I thought it was Vinland."

"Finland?" said Ginger.

"Don't you remember doing a Viking project when you were in Ms Arthur's class?" said Carrie.

"No," said Ginger. "I was in Mr Williams' class and we did Roman Britain. I've done that three times now."

"Well, I think Vinland is what the Vikings called America," said Alex.

"They went to America?" said Ginger.

"Yes, well, Canada I think it was," said Alex. "They sailed from Greenland. What was the name of that chap, Carrie, the one who was the son of Erik the Red?"

"Leif Eriksson," said Carrie.

"Leif the Lucky, they're calling him now," said Magnus' father, who had overheard them. "So, his fame has spread to your land, has it?" He eyed them shrewdly. "And have you heard of me? I'm Leif the Hospitable!" He laughed again and clapped them on the shoulders with a huge hand like a leg of pork. "Come back to our house with the children and join in our feast. We can swap travellers' tales."

"I don't think he's going to accept us as easily as

the children," said Cedric, as they followed the straggling trail of sailors and villagers back to the wood and turf settlement. As they got closer they could smell cooking fires and hear dogs barking wildly as they recognised their returning masters.

"No," agreed Alex, reluctantly. "I suppose we'd better move on."

"Must we?" pleaded Carrie. "I want to see if my model was right."

"All right, but we'd better not stay after that."

It was a mistake. The children got swept up in the crowd of homecomers and welcomers. The whole village seemed to be having a spontaneous street party. Not that it really had streets, just rutted mud lanes, but these were quite hard because of the cold. Fires were soon lit in the open space in the middle, meat was roasting, wine and ale were brought and drunk from horn cups. Someone started to play a kind of harp and everyone began to sing. Alex, Carrie and Ginger, jostled by all the rejoicing Vikings felt a bit out of it. It wasn't their fathers who had come home and they didn't know the words of the song.

Suddenly, from out of the dancing, laughing crowd, came the bearlike figure of Leif Magnusson.

"Ah, my little travellers," he bellowed, a full cup of something spilling in his hand. "Come and join our revels. You must eat and drink with us to celebrate our safe return from a perilous voyage." He thrust the cup into Alex's hand and made him drink.

"Thanks," spluttered Alex, coughing as the strong drink burned his throat. "I think we'd better be getting back actually. Our parents will be wondering where we are."

It was a very silly thing for a supposedly intrepid voyager to say. But then he did something even sillier. He looked at his watch.

Leif looked at it dumbfounded. It was a large-faced digital watch with the Hearts of Midlothian emblem on the face. Even to Alex it looked alien and not remotely Viking.

"What is that?" asked Leif, lifting Alex's wrist in his huge hairy hand.

"Cedric," whispered Ginger, "do something!"

He pulled Alex's hand out of the Viking's, grabbed it and Carrie's and hoped hard that Cedric was doing the spell. A frenzied squeaking followed and then the brown and green village faded till it looked like the negative of a photograph. The children just noticed the snow closing in on them and then there was nothing but the swirling sensation of travelling through hundreds of years in seconds.

5

Going West

When the world stopped spinning, the whirling lights in the children's vision were replaced by a monotonous drumming in their ears. At first they thought the sound was more of the aftermath of leaping through time. But gradually, as their eyes became accustomed to their new environment, they found that the noise was if anything getting louder. Nothing they could see could account for it. They were on a wide plain. Grassland stretched out around them, so parched and yellow it looked for an instant as if they were back in the Egyptian desert.

In the distance was a line of blue hills. The sun was high in the sky and the children soon had to strip off their sweatshirts.

"Cedric!" complained Alex. "Why is it that wherever we end up, we're always too hot or too cold?"

Cedric opened and shut his mouth a few times, but could find no suitable reply. Ginger looked around with interest.

"This isn't the war either, is it?" he said.

Carrie looked disappointed. She was beginning to feel that she would never see Beauty again. She had got over losing the ghost cat very well, but when Alex had told her his idea for a birthday present, she couldn't help remembering how lovely it had been to bury her face in the tortoiseshell's long neck fur and listen to the deep motor in her throat. It had been quite fun seeing the ancient Egyptians and the Vikings, though the dinosaurs had been a bit too alarming. But this place, wherever it was, was even more desolate than Greenland. There was no sign of any animals. And what was that strange thrumming that made the ground vibrate?

The children raised their heads at the same time and saw them, coming over the horizon. Hundreds and hundreds of them. One huge mass of muscle and horn, galloping, snorting, kicking up the dust of the dry grassland. Buffalo. The children were transfixed. There was nowhere to run, nowhere to hide. There was nothing but the plains and a huge herd of buffalo heading straight towards them.

"Run!" screamed Carrie, and they ran. But it was useless. The buffalo ran faster than they could and were gaining on them by the minute. Alex wondered wildly if they could be killed in a time where they didn't really exist. It was like the worst

kind of nightmare, where your legs won't obey your brain and the menace is right behind you and about to catch up. The noise was unimaginable: deafening hoof beats of hundreds of pounds of animal strength, punctuated by snorts and bellows.

As the stampeding herd came right up behind the stumbling, fleeing children, Carrie thought she could hear human shouts among the animal noises. But then her nostrils filled with the strong smell of wild buffalo and she felt the heat of their breath on her neck and she could think of nothing but being trampled to death. Suddenly she was snatched up into the air. She thought for one dizzy moment that one of the huge snorting animals had tossed her up on its horns. Then she realised that she had landed across the neck of a piebald horse and was being gripped by the strong arm of a Native American.

Ginger was running as he never had in his life before. He was terrified of bulls. To be honest, he was terrified of cows and would never enter a field if there was even the mildest of old milkers in it. A stampeding herd of buffalo inches behind him was his idea of hell. When the brave leant down at full gallop and swept him across his horse's neck, Ginger didn't realise what had happened. He thought he had fainted. Then he looked up and saw the plaited hair, the feather in the headband and the scars on the handsome face of his captor. Ginger fainted.

Alex merely thought that Cedric had done another quick time-travelling spell when he found himself flying through the air. It was only when he saw the ground moving fast beneath him instead of all round him that he realised he was inside the buffalo herd instead of in front of it.

The three natives peeled off from the main

group of buffalo hunters and gradually slackened speed. Many others stayed with the animals, looking for an opportunity to kill one with their arrows. The children's three captors wheeled round and came to a halt, talking rapidly to one another as their horses snorted and pranced, unaccustomed to being suddenly pulled out of a hunt. Gradually the children realised that they had all been saved from certain death.

Words suddenly gained meaning above their heads and they realised, thanks to Cedric's translation spell, that they were being discussed. Even Ginger listened, though his eyes were fixed in terror the whole time on the tomahawk in his captor's belt.

"They are only children," said Alex's brave.

"But children of the whiteskins," said Carrie's.

"Soldier's children, maybe," said Ginger's.

"No," laughed Alex's, feeling his jacket, "look at their clothes. They wear rough overalls like ranchers."

"Or like those who come in search of gold," said Carrie's.

"Let us take these little gold-seekers back to

camp," said Ginger's brave. "Old Bear will know what to do with them."

And before they could form any idea of who Old Bear might be, the children were clinging on to the manes of their rescuers' horses as they galloped rapidly away from the buffalo and toward the blue hills. It seemed only minutes before they were in the foothills, rushing towards an encampment of tipis around a small stream. The women and children and some older men had been left behind when the braves went on the buffalo hunt and now they hurried away from their cooking fires at the sight of three of their young men galloping towards them with unexpected booty across their horses' necks.

The braves slid easily off their horses, keeping hold of the children in an iron grip. They frog-marched them towards a large tipi in the centre of the camp, more ornately decorated than the rest. Alex was firmly handed over to the young man who held Carrie, and his brave ducked under the entrance flap of what was obviously the home of Old Bear.

But when the Chief came out after the brave, they saw to their surprise that he was not old at all. He was tall and strong and only a few years older than the brave he followed. Alex suddenly knew with certainty that this Chief would have rather been out on the buffalo hunt than safe at home in his tipi. He welcomed this unexpected diversion from boredom. Alex tried to bow, which was difficult in his position, and signalled to the others to do the same.

"Greetings, Mighty Chief," he improvised. "We thank Old Bear and his tribe for saving us from the buffalo."

The Chief bent down to look at his captives, the huge eagle feather in the back of his headband curving over his black hair. He signalled to the braves to let go of them.

"Greetings, whiteskin children. Tell me where you are from and how you appeared among the buffalo. Are you spirits?"

Carrie, who was best at geography, said:

"We are from far in the North and East, O Chief. We are not spirits, but lost children who want to go home."

"Iroquois," muttered the braves, but Chief Old Bear lifted his right hand.

"They are not of the people. That is clear. When did you ever see Mohawk or Dakota the colour of this one." He took a handful of Ginger's long floppy hair and pulled back to get a better look at his face. "He looks like a red dog."

Ginger, terrified of this interest in his unruly locks, cried out: "Cedric, help! They're going to scalp me."

Old Bear frowned and let go of Ginger's fringe.

"We do not scalp babies," he said sternly. "Even ones who do not tell us the truth. You, Cedric," he said, pointing at Alex. "You must tell me. Are you spies from the army? One of their leaders has red dog hair like this snivelling coward. Is it his father?"

"No," said Alex, truthfully. "My friend's father is far, far away. We are all a long way from our parents and none of them have anything to do with any army."

"You know the soldiers want to take the land from us though?" asked Old Bear. "All whiteskins want to take what is not theirs."

"I know," said Carrie unexpectedly. "And I don't think it's right. You were here first, weren't you?"

"This is a wise child," said Old Bear. Suddenly he relaxed and laughed and the three braves laughed with him. "I don't know what to do with these three rabbits you found in the grass," said the Chief. "If the whiteskin soldiers find we have children of their kind, they will say we kidnapped them and use it as another excuse to attack us. If we just let them go and they really are lost, they may die on the plains. They've already nearly been trampled and clearly have no survival skills or woodcraft."

Suddenly there was a loud rumbling sound, almost like the buffalo stampede. It was Ginger's stomach and his face became the colour of his hair. The Chief laughed even more.

"But they are only children. And children must be fed. I hear the hunt returning. There will soon be meat for all."

It was not long before the children were sitting round the cooking fire of Old Bear himself. Darkness was falling and the orange flames leapt up, hissing as fat from the chunks of buffalo meat dripped on to the fire. The Chief stood up and began a long prayer of thanks.

"Saying grace," whispered Ginger to Carrie and Alex.

"O Great Spirit," said the Chief, and all the people round all the fires waited, listening to him. "We thank you for the success of the hunt, which has brought us much fresh meat. O Spirit of the

Buffalo, we thank you for your flesh to eat, which will fill us with your strength and vigour. We thank you for your skin, which will give us tipis and moccasins and saddles and even your sinews, which will string our bows and sew our garments. We pledge ourselves to use all the great gifts you give us, to waste nothing and to remember you with respect, gratitude and much honour as we accept these your blessings..."

The children looked at one another guiltily. This was a long way from McDonald's. At last the prayer came to an end and Old Bear handed them each a chunk of steaming, savoury meat. Carrie hesitated. She was practically a vegetarian.

"Go on," hissed Alex. "Otherwise the buffalo will have died for nothing." Carrie nodded, swallowed and took a large bite. The boys did the same.

At that moment, a fusillade of shots went off around the camp and all the men leapt to their feet, overturning cooking pots and putting out fires. They grabbed their bows and slung their quivers over their shoulders. The children were shoved roughly towards a tipi. They felt utterly helpless and soon felt even more so as the familiar rushing sound around them told them that Cedric was doing another time-travelling spell. As they began to whirl away, Alex locked eyes with Old Bear, who was shouting orders to his men. "It wasn't us!" called Alex. "We had nothing to do with it!"

But the Chief only stared in wonder as the three children disappeared from his time and place for ever.

6

Black and Gold

When the rushing stopped and the children found themselves in a jungle clearing, they took no notice of their surroundings for some time. They were all too upset by the scene they had just left. Together they tried to share the little they knew about what had happened between the Native Americans and the US Army.

"Didn't they win a big battle at Little Bighorn?" asked Alex.

"Yeah," said Ginger. "That was Custard's last stand."

"Custer," said Carrie. "He was the army General. He and all his men got killed."

"But wasn't there another time, called Wounded Knee," said Alex. "When the soldiers murdered loads of Indians?"

"Native Americans," corrected Carrie. "It was the white settlers who called them Indians. It was because Christopher Columbus thought he'd discovered India."

"How come you know so much about it?" demanded Ginger, who had been considerably shaken by his experience on the western plains.

"I don't know anything," said Carrie crossly. "I feel so ignorant. I don't even know if Old Bear's tribe survived that attack. I don't like all this going back in the past. I want to go home."

Alex got Cedric out of his pocket. "What do you say, Cedric? We didn't get a peep out of you in the encampment. Shall we give up trying to find Beauty?"

"And where are we now, as a matter of interest?" asked Ginger, looking around him for the first time.

"One question at a time," said Cedric primly. "I don't think we should give up on Beauty yet. I added another spell involving locating a cat.

72

Admittedly this does not look like wartime London, but I have a very strong sense that we are close to one of the animals who came back to us from the past at Ferry Road."

It did not look like London in the Blitz. The clearing was floored with emerald-green grass. The trees around it were a kind the children didn't recognise, hung with vines and creepers. There was a sudden movement in the leaves.

"Look!" gasped Carrie. "It's a monkey."

It was a whole troop of monkeys, whooping and swinging through the trees, as free and wild as birds.

"How lovely," said Carrie, quite cheered up. "I've never seen so many at once."

"Definitely not London,"

said Ginger.

As soon as the troop of monkeys had gone, their sounds were replaced by distant human shouts. The children looked wearily at one another. They had already encountered Egyptian camel drivers, Viking explorers and Native Americans, not to mention dinosaurs, and were getting a bit wary of who they might meet next. So far nothing very terrible had actually happened, but they kept thinking it was going to.

"Never fear," said Cedric, reading their minds, "I've always got you out of danger so far, haven't I?"

At that moment an Indian broke through the trees. A real one, in a loincloth and a turban, not a Native American. He was followed by several others, carrying spears and nets. He was as astonished to see the children as they were to see him. He turned and called back into the depths of the jungle.

"Sahib! Sahib! Colonel Sahib! We have found something!"

A man in khaki uniform with a moustache, wearing one of those tropical hats called a solar topi, and looking strangely familiar, strode into the clearing.

"It's Colonel Kinnear," gasped Carrie, recognising the figure they had last seen in an old sepia photograph from the Ferry Road attic.

The Colonel halted, puzzled.

"That's right, young feller," he said. "But how do you know me? You look like pukka British children, but why are you dressed like ragamuffins? And what are you doing in the middle of my tiger hunt?"

"Tiger hunt!" exclaimed Alex.

"Oh dear! I think I must have locked on to the wrong cat," whispered Cedric, who had again retreated to the safety of Alex's pocket.

The Colonel was having a hurried consultation with his head beater. He turned back to the children.

"All right, we've decided to abandon the hunt for today. No sign of stripes anyway. You had better come back with me and we'll see what the Mem Sahibs make of you. Can't expect a bachelor like me to start playing nursemaid, what? Mahout!

Bring Rajah out here."

The children watched fascinated as the trees parted and a massive grey head poked through the leaves. Carrie clutched Alex's arm.

"You don't think that's the one who..." she whispered.

"No," Alex whispered back. "The Colonel wouldn't shoot his own elephant! He probably picked up that revolting umbrella stand in some bazaar or other."

They both remembered the angry ghost elephant that had materialised in their hallway and had been exorcised by Mungo, as the much calmer beast Rajah lumbered forward and knelt down in front of the Colonel.

"Up you go then," said Colonel Kinnear to the three children. "Mind how you go. Plenty of room in the howdah."

One by one they stepped on the massive animal's forefeet and, guided by the mahout, climbed on to its shoulder and into a construction that was a cross between a cable car and a brightly decorated little house. The elephant shifted nervously

and flickered its small eyes when Alex climbed aboard.

"Perhaps it knows you've got a mouse in your pocket," whispered Ginger, but not quietly enough.

As the elephant straightened up and began its stately march back through the jungle, the Colonel, who was sitting next to Carrie, leaned forward in the howdah and said to Alex:

"Got a mouse with you, young feller? Let's see."

Alex froze. Was he to show Cedric to this man with a gun who shot tigers and rhinos? What would he do?

"Go on," said Carrie, "show the Colonel. But keep hold of him. You don't want Rajah to know he's loose."

Alex gently drew Cedric out of his pocket. The Colonel put out a huge forefinger and stroked the little mouse gently.

"What a dear little chap," said the Colonel. "I used to keep white mice myself, you know, when I was a boy. Great little companions. Clean, intelligent, friendly. Can't think why my sisters didn't like them."

"My sister likes Cedric," said Alex, winking at Carrie, but he didn't let on that she was the sister in question.

"I don't understand," said Ginger. "If you like animals, why do you want to kill them?"

"What sort of fool question is that?" said the Colonel, turning red in the face. "Shooting big game is sport. It hasn't got anything to do with liking or not liking animals."

"But it has," said Carrie. "You could take photographs of them instead. Lots of big-game hunters do. They realise how few of the animals are left."

"What rot!" said the Colonel. "The jungle's teeming with 'em. Photographs indeed. I never heard such poppycock."

"Carrie," hissed Alex. "Remember what Mungo said about changing things."

The elephant arrived at an impressive white house on the edge of the jungle and the children dismounted. They were handed over to a servant in a white uniform with a gleaming white turban. The whole house was full of servants, carrying out different duties. The white-turbanned one was called Hari and he found some cool white clothes for the boys. Unlike the Colonel, he knew straight-away that Carrie was a girl, in spite of her short hair, and gave her into the care of an ayah, who dressed her in a blue and silver sari with a short blue blouse like a croptop underneath.

When they joined the Colonel for dinner in his ornate dining-room, his jaw dropped.

"Well here's a fine kettle of fish," he said. "You never said one of you was a little Mem Sahib all along. What a hoyden, dressing up in boy's clothes and playing in the jungle! Well, Major Fitzallen is coming over for tiffin tomorrow morning and he's going to bring Mrs Fitzallen with him. She'll know what to do. In the meantime, sit down and eat. Children are always hungry, aren't they?"

"That's what the Dakota thought too," said Ginger quietly.

But the Colonel didn't go in for a long prayer to the spirits of his food animals. A short, Anglican grace was soon over and they were spooning up a delicious spicy soup called Mulligatawny. The children found that they were incredible hungry. Their mouths had been watering over their first bites of buffalo when Cedric had whisked them away from America to India and they couldn't remember when they had last eaten before.

The soup was followed by rice, lentils, flat rounds of bread, six different chutneys and pickles in silver bowls and several steaming dishes of hot curry. The children ate it all. They were all used to spicy food from the many restaurants and carry outs of Edinburgh. The Colonel watched in astonishment as they cleaned their plates and asked for second helpings. The servants beamed and heaped their plates with everything they wanted.

"That was brilliant, Colonel, thank you," said Alex, when he was full to bursting.

"Don't mention it," said the Colonel. "My pleasure. I must say it quite gives a fellow an appetite to see the way you chaps fall to it. It's a bit dull sitting here of an evening facing all this on my own, you know."

After delicious little cone-shaped ice-creams, stuck with pistachio nuts, the children were led into another room and soon joined by the Colonel. He was holding a large balloon-shaped glass.

"Seems a bit silly to drink my chota peg of brandy all alone in the dining-room when I could have some company," he said. "Hari, let the dogs in, will you?"

Two Dalmatians came running in joyfully and, after a quick lick at their master's hands, set to diligent sniffing of the newcomers.

"These are my usual companions," said the Colonel. "This is Dotty, short for Dorothy, and this is Dapple."

Alex and Ginger fussed over the dogs, but Carrie was staring in horror at a rug; it was a tiger rug, complete with head, the mouth fixed open in a menacing snarl. Carrie grasped the Colonel by the hand, as he gazed fondly at his dogs.

"How could you?" she cried, her voice choking.

"It was beautiful and alive and now it's just a hearthrug!"

"Steady on, old girl," said the Colonel uncomfortably, trying not to spill his drink.

"Yes, steady on," said Alex, adding in a whisper. "It's not our tiger. It's much too big."

Carrie glared at him.

"What does that matter!" she hissed. "It was somebody's tiger. It was its *own* tiger." Then she burst into tears and ran out of the room.

Much later the three children were lying on campbeds under mosquito nets in a large cool bedroom with windows opening on to a veranda. Alex had stretched a point and implied they were two brothers and a sister in order for them all to share a room. He was worried about Carrie. She had got herself into such a state and he didn't know if she could get an asthma attack in the past. He was also worried that she was going to do something that would alter the future.

Ginger was asleep and snoring. He had eaten a whole plate of sweetmeats after dinner. Alex was wide awake, with Cedric on the pillow beside him. He knew that Carrie couldn't sleep either.

"Cedric," he whispered. "We're not in any danger, but I think we're going to have to get away from here before Carrie does something she shouldn't."

"I think you're right," agreed the mouse.

"And another thing," said Alex. "If we don't make it to see Beauty soon, I think we'll have to give it up. I didn't want to give Carrie a birthday present that would upset her."

The hot night was full of the small sounds of the jungle – rustlings in the leaves, the whirring of insects and croaking of frogs. Then suddenly there came a deep coughing sound. Carrie flung off her mosquito net and ran out on to the veranda.

"It's our tiger. I know it is. I've got to warn her. Or the Colonel will shoot her." And she ran off into the garden before Alex could stop her.

7

Blitz!

Alex shook Ginger awake and explained the situation as quickly as he could. Stuffing Cedric into his pyjama pocket, he ran out into the garden, calling Carrie. But he had lost precious minutes. The jungle met the garden of the Colonel's residence right outside its walls, and Carrie had already been swallowed up in its shadows. Alex stood staring out into the jungle, his heart pounding. Carrie was out there, looking for a tiger she thought would recognise her as a friend and ally. But here in the past, in India, the tiger was just a wild creature, who had not yet been summoned to twentieth-century

Britain by Cedric.

Carrie's most likely fate would be a horrible mauling, or even death, if that could happen in the past. But if somehow she did succeed in communicating with the tiger and warning it to stay away from Colonel Kinnear, then she would have changed the future in just the way Mungo had warned against. Either way, Alex had to find her and quickly. But nothing would be gained by plunging wildly off into the jungle, except perhaps his own death.

He had a sudden horrible thought. What if the Colonel had shot the tiger because it had killed two children he had found wandering in the jungle?

"Sorry I took so long," came Ginger's breathless voice. He had changed back into his twentieth-century clothes and he had brought Alex's and Carrie's with him in a bundle. "I figured we'd be leaving as soon as we catch up with Carrie," he said.

Ginger's common sense brought Alex back to his senses. He changed quickly into his jeans and jacket, carefully transferring Cedric, and gathered up Carrie's clothes.

"Cedric, if we find Carrie, can you get us out of here?" he asked.

"I think so," said the little mouse. "I've modified the animal-tracking spell and I think I really can lock on to Beauty this time."

"Well, stay alert," said Alex.

"Can't you use another spell to locate the tiger?" said Ginger.

Cedric's white fur seemed to turn paler in the moonlight.

"I suppose I could. But wouldn't that be frightfully dangerous?"

"It's our only chance of getting close to Carrie out in that jungle," said Alex.

"Yeah," said Ginger. "Think of her, all alone out there, trying to talk to a wild tiger!"

Cedric closed his eyes and muttered. "OK," he said. "This way..."

The two boys climbed stealthily over the wall, leaving Alex's white pyjamas lying on the grass like a discarded chrysalis. Inside the house, Dotty and Dapple pricked up their ears, but knowing there

were no strangers in the garden, subsided again at the foot of the Colonel's bed.

In a clearing in the jungle Carrie's white night-gown fluttered like a moth against the dark trunks of the peepul trees. She was horribly afraid. It had seemed so simple when she first heard the tiger. But now, alone in the night, in a jungle that was not just thousands of miles from home but about a hundred years as well, it was altogether different. She wished for the millionth time that she'd waited for Alex and Ginger. The jungle was full of sounds and any one of them could have been the soft swish of a big cat pushing through the leaves on its huge tawny paws. Carrie remembered riding that tiger, if indeed it was the same one, through the streets of Edinburgh. It had been a magnificent beast.

"I must save it," thought Carrie. "I must be brave."

The soft coughing came again. Through the trees across the clearing Carrie saw it, black and gold stripes gleaming in the moonlight. It stopped and looked at her, its amber eyes blank with the incomprehensible stare of a cat. Carrie froze.

"Now!" said Alex, and Carrie had just time to realise that a boy had grabbed each of her arms before they all started their dizzying whirl through time and space.

When she was aware of her surroundings, Carrie found herself shivering in her muslin nightgown. They seemed to be in a sort of underground tunnel. Alex handed Carrie her warm clothes and she changed quickly.

"Thanks," she said quietly. "I mean thanks for

saving me." They both knew that she was thinking of the tiger, who had not been saved, and was on its way to its pointless death as a hunting trophy.

"Where are we now?" asked Ginger briskly.

"We are in London in the 1940s," announced Cedric triumphantly.

"Really?" said Alex. "No kidding? That's great. But how do we find Beauty?"

"There are people lying down a bit further along," said Ginger, peering into the gloom. "Come on, let's go that way."

By the time they reached the huddled figures, some light was filtering down into the tunnel. People were beginning to sit up, yawning and stretching. Alex looked at a sign on the tiled wall of the tunnel. It said MORNINGTON CRESCENT.

"It's the underground," he whispered to the others. "Don't you remember that people used to sleep on the underground platforms during the air-raids in London?"

They followed the stream of tired Londoners up the steps into the morning light. No one looked at them twice. Each person had the grey, exhausted face of those who go to work each day after not enough sleep on a cold hard floor. The children emerged blinking in the pale light of early morning and gasped at what they saw. None of them had been to London before and their knowledge of the city was based on films and TV series, which always showed Big Ben or the bright lights of Piccadilly Circus. What they saw outside Mornington Crescent station was a row of shops and houses with a gaping hole in the middle.

Smoke and brick dust were still rising off the heap of rubble that had once been someone's house and probably their business too. On the walls of the houses that still stood on either side, you could see the pattern of the wallpaper in the demolished rooms and even, incredibly, a picture still hanging on a hook, its glass shattered. Outside, firemen and ARP wardens in tin hats were milling around organising wooden props to shore up the neighbouring houses. One of the underground sleepers stopped to talk to a warden.

"Direct hit?" he asked.

"Yes," said the warden. "Jerry was busy last night.

We had about half a dozen on our patch alone."

"Who's Jerry?" whispered Ginger. "Is he a bomber?"

"It's what they called the Germans," said Carrie.

"Message for whoever's in charge here," came a voice from behind the children that sounded just like home. They turned and saw a soldier in uniform. He was as carroty-haired as Ginger, with freckles and a big grin, in spite of the horrible mess he was looking at. Directed by the warden, he went over to a tall man with a silver moustache.

"That must be him," said Carrie.

"Who?" asked Alex.

"Beauty's master," she said. "You remember Beauty said her master was in the war. And you heard how he sounded. He had a Scottish accent. I bet he took Beauty back home with him when the war was over and that's how she ended up in Ferry Road."

"So, if we just follow him around all day" said Ginger, "we should find Beauty?"

"Sounds foolproof to me," said Alex.

But following a soldier round wartime London was harder than it seemed. The children often wanted to ask Cedric to go back to the vanishing spell. The only thing that stopped them was a strong sense that it would be dangerous to be under the influence of two such strong spells as time travel and invisibility at the same time.

The soldier had a busy day, visiting many different bombsites and returning to his headquarters in between. His duties were obviously concerned with civilian casualties and damage to buildings more than direct military action. Several times he looked round uneasily, as if he was aware of being followed. But three grubby children look much like any other three in the eyes of a preoccupied grown-up, and it was nearly dark before the soldier had enough time to be sure there really *was* someone following him. He was coming off duty from his headquarters when he took the children by surprise as they waited outside for him.

"Hey!" he said, grabbing Ginger by the wrist as the three of them were about to make a run for it. "What is it with you three? You've been following

me, haven't you? What's it all about."

Before the boys could stop her, Carrie came out
with the truth.

"We're looking for a cat. A long-haired tortoiseshell called Beauty. We thought you might know
where she was."

It had a magical effect on the soldier. He was a
kind man and he relaxed.

"Oh I see," he said. "You've lost your cat. I
understand. I'm very fond of cats myself. But I'm
afraid I haven't seen her. At least I don't think so.

You get lots of strays and lost pets roaming the bombsites. They mostly run away from people. But I don't think I've seen one of that description."

The children looked at one another. How could they be wrong about the soldier? The black-out curtains were being pulled in people's houses and they realised that although it was getting dark outside, no streetlights were going on. The soldier looked at his watch.

"You shouldn't be out this late," he said. "Your parents will be worrying. Tell me where you live and I'll walk you home."

The children wondered what they could possibly say. Then there came a blood-curdling noise that they had all heard on old war films. It was the sound of an air-raid siren wailing very close to them. The soldier looked alarmed.

"Quick, we must get into a shelter!" he said, looking round for a likely safe place. They were walking past a corner house and he ducked down the side street and was back in an instant.

"Down here, quickly," he ordered them. "There's a shelter in this garden."

"Won't the people mind?" asked Carrie, as he marched them briskly down the road and into someone's back garden through their gate. The soldier gave her an odd look. The family didn't seem to be there anyway. There was no one else in the shelter as they climbed in. Ginger was the last before the soldier, but he stopped in the doorway.

"Hurry up," urged the soldier, "the bombers will be here any minute."

"But isn't that Beauty?" said Ginger. "Hiding under that bush?" He dived into a flowerbed and scooped up an armful of hissing, scratching tortoiseshell, just as the soldier flung him into the shelter and top-

pled in on top of him. Just in time. The children, huddled on campbeds in the dark damp shelter, heard an ear-splitting thump louder than any noise they had ever heard before. There was no doubt in their minds that it was a German bomb.

8

Children of the Stars

The vibrations from the bomb and the sound of falling bricks continued for many minutes. Ginger had been badly scratched by Beauty who was now crouched with flattened ears under one of the campbeds. When the silence eventually returned, everyone realised that they had been clenching their teeth and holding their breath. A joint sigh whispered round the shelter as they exhaled.

"Whew!" said the soldier. "I guess you could say that one didn't have our numbers on it. Though I wouldn't want to cut it as close as that again."

"Chocolate, anyone?" said Alex, bringing out his battered rations.

Ginger and Carrie had some rather squashed bars to add to the feast and the atmosphere in the shelter soon had the party feeling of survivors everywhere.

"Well, you found your cat anyway," said the soldier. "Even if she didn't seem very grateful."

Beauty had been coaxed out and was now sitting on Carrie's lap being stroked. Alex and Ginger looked at one another with a silent grin of victory. After all their mad leaps through time and space they were here at the right time and the right place. Carrie had her birthday present at last. In the dark, Alex had eased the terrified Cedric out of his pocket and was surreptitiously feeding him crumbs of chocolate to revive him.

"Well done, Cedric," he whispered. "Just look at Carrie!"

"Is there something wrong with your sister?" asked the soldier. "She seems to be crying."

Alex produced a pocket torch and shone it on Carrie. The soldier was right. Her eyes were red and swollen and her nose was running.

"Just happy to see Beauty again," said Ginger,

hoping it was true.

"It might be shock," said the soldier, concerned. "It often takes people like that after a near miss. I wonder if it's safe to go out yet. We should get her some medical treatment, or at least some sweet tea."

Alex looked closely at Carrie. The unmistakable wheezing was beginning. But Carrie *was* crying too.

"It doesn't work," she whispered to Alex. "Beauty isn't a ghost any more. She's real and fluffy and it's making my asthma start."

It was true. Alex cursed himself for being such an idiot. He had been so full of his plans for Carrie's birthday surprise and so excited that they seemed to have worked at last that he had never thought beyond his sister's happy reunion with the tortoiseshell cat. Because Carrie had been able to cuddle the ghost of Beauty without any ill effects in the present, Alex had stupidly assumed it would be the same in the past. But it wasn't. This Beauty was all too real and Alex now had to save Carrie from his own birthday present

"Perhaps you could take a look outside?" he suggested to the soldier, his mind racing.

"Sure thing," said the soldier, opening the shelter door. "I'll just have a quick recce. Back in a tick." He was gone.

"Quick, Cedric," said Alex. "You've got to get the spell right first time and get us back home."

Cedric began to flex his paws.

"No, wait," said Alex, looking at Carrie. "Not

here. Take us straight to the infirmary. And, Carrie, you must put Beauty down. You can't take her with us."

As Carrie reluctantly put the cat down, Ginger muttered, "It's taken us six goes to get here. What makes you think he can aim for a place as well as a time?"

Then the whirling began and the children were no longer in the shelter.

"What will the soldier think?" wheezed Carrie as they spun through the years.

"I don't know," gasped Alex, his hair flying. "But I reckon he'll look after Beauty."

"He did make it to the hospital," said Ginger in amazement as the spinning stopped and they found themselves in a gleaming white room full of complicated machines and instruments. Carrie was lying on a state-of-the-art hospital bed, still wheezing and choking.

"I think the infirmary must have had a bit of a refit," said Alex cautiously, looking round at the banks of consoles. "This looks more like a spaceship

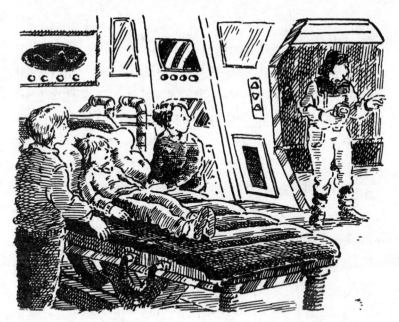

than an examination room."

Just then a person backed into the room talking to someone outside. "I'll just get a..." she said, then stopped, surprised to find the room occupied. She pursed her lips in annoyance and went straight over to Carrie.

"That triage droid's done it again," she said to the boys, concentrating all her attention on Carrie. "Transported a patient through without bleeping me."

The doctor, for that was obviously what she was,

was wearing white, but not just the usual crumpled cotton jacket. She was dressed from top to toe in a shiny white jump-suit made of a material that looked as if it would repel all dirt and stains. She didn't use a stethoscope but held a small machine in her hand which she passed over Carrie's chest.

"Just like Star Trek," whispered Ginger.

The doctor looked puzzled and turned to the boys. "Where are you from? All my readings are telling me that the child has a condition that died out on earth nearly a hundred years ago. Are you from some community on a satellite I don't know about?" She looked them up and down. "You certainly don't look as if you're from round here."

"It's asthma," said Alex. "She was cuddling a cat."

"That was my diagnosis," said the doctor. "But why hasn't she been given Pneumatron?"

Alex and Ginger had no answer to that. The doctor moved briskly to one of the consoles and pressed a few buttons. A metal instrument slid smoothly out into a collection compartment. The doctor took it and pressed it against Carrie's neck.

Almost instantly the wheezing stopped and Carrie was able to sit up.

"Brilliant," said Alex. "She's never recovered so quickly. Er, when exactly was Pneumatron invented?"

"2010," said the doctor briskly. "Asthma was a real plague at the end of the twentieth century, because of the pollution. But the combination of the drug and the Global Clean Air Act wiped the condition out in under a decade. I don't know where you guys have been hiding that could have produced a case like this in 2096!"

"2096!" mouthed Ginger. "Oh, Cedric!"

"How long will it last?" said Carrie, swinging her legs off the table.

"Last?" said the doctor, laughing. "It's a permanent cure. One dose of the strength you've just had will ensure that the condition never returns." She walked over to the door. "I just need to get the admissions cartridge off that dopey droid and then I can discharge you."

The children were not going to risk the doctor finding out that no breathless girl had been admitted. They waited two minutes then crept down the corridor after the doctor. Much more dodging behind pillars brought them to the exit, where the doctor was in hot dispute with a metal receptionist. They sneaked out through doors which not only opened automatically but said "Have a nice day!" as they passed through. Instinctively, they decided to put as much distance between them and the hospital as possible.

It was night-time in the twenty-first century and the sky was full of stars, but there was something unfamiliar about them. Every so often there was a large bright light that seemed much closer to the earth. And occasionally a strange spacecraft would pass through the night sky, its sleek lines picked out in lights. The streets and apartment buildings were all unrecognisable and the cars and buses ran silently, some on the road and some along elevated highways. The air was clear and unpolluted.

They stopped in a sort of park that was vaguely familiar.

"Look!" said Ginger. "There's Arthur's Seat. We *are* in Edinburgh."

"Yes," said Alex, taking Cedric in his hand. "Right place, Cedric, even down to the hospital. Just a hundred years too late."

"I hope you're not complaining," said Cedric indignantly. "I got Carrie cured, didn't I?"

They had to admit he had.

"But will it still work when we get back home?" asked Carrie anxiously.

"I don't really know," said the little mouse quietly. The children were astonished. Cedric never admitted not knowing anything. "You know what Mungo said about tampering with the past," said Cedric. "I don't know if the same thing applies to tampering with the future."

"Well," said Alex, "there's only one way to find out. Cedric, it really is time to go home."

Alex's bedroom had never seemed so welcoming. Even the scattered clothes that should have been put into the laundry basket and the apple core on the window sill that had been there for a week and was beginning to turn furry. The children came to in an untidy heap in the middle of the floor, a split second before Mrs Brodie put her head round the door.

"Oh there you all are. Dad and I are just popping out to the supermarket, but Mungo's in the house if you need anyone." She stopped and looked at them. "I don't know what you've been doing, but you look as if you've been dragged through a hedge backwards. Do try and tidy yourselves up a bit."

"Yes, Mum," "Yes, Mrs Brodie," they chorused automatically as she left the room.

"Well done, Cedric," said Ginger. "You really pulled it off."

The tiny mouse yawned a huge pink yawn.

"I'm utterly exhausted," he said. "Alex, please put me in my bedding." Alex gently tucked him in among his curls of shredded paper and the little creature fell fast asleep.

"What I don't understand," said Carrie. "Is how he could get it right just now when he couldn't before?"

Alex put his finger to his lips. "He didn't," he whispered. "Don't ever tell him, but I used Mungo's word of power."

A few days later the children were gathered in Mungo's attic having an impromptu celebration party. The guest of honour was Cedric who sat beside a cereal bowl full of chocolate raisins, sunflowerseeds and cashew nuts. Carrie had been for a routine check-up to Dr Murdoch and he had found to his astonishment that her asthma had completely disappeared.

"They do sometimes grow out of it at Carrie's age," he had told her delighted parents, "but I've never had a case where it happened so suddenly."

Carrie had made sure not to leave the surgery without getting Dr Murdoch to agree there was no reason why the Brodies shouldn't have a cat.

"So I might be getting a kitten for Christmas," Carrie told Mungo, beaming all over her face, "and it's all thanks to Cedric." She leaned over and planted a careful kiss between his little round ears. The white mouse turned pink.

"And," said Alex, "I've already opened negotiations for a dog – though they did say a wolfhound would be too big."

"That is splendid news," said Mungo. "No more need for ghost animals and no more need to travel back in time."

"Sounds like no more fun," said Ginger gloomily. He was pleased for his friends but he had got used to the excitement of Cedric's erratic magic.

"I wouldn't say that," said Mungo. "I'm thinking of taking on an apprentice. And he'll need to experiment a little."

Cedric pricked up his ears. "Do you mean me?"

"No, Cedric," said Mungo gently. "I think your experiences in time travel should have taught you the difference between a familiar and an apprentice. I need you to help me with my magic. But I also need someone I can train, someone who will himself need a familiar."

They all turned and looked at Alex. He was

blushing too. He had told Mungo about the word of power and had been praised for keeping his head, but he hadn't expected this honour.

"Do you still want to be an astronaut?" asked Mungo.

"Not as much as I want to be a magician," said Alex.

"Then let's shake hands on it," said Mungo. "After all, we already share a familiar." He raised his mug of tea. "And now a toast," he declared. "To magic!"

"To magic," said the children and the mouse.

"And to Cedric," added Alex.

"To Cedric! " cried all the humans. "A mouse in a million."